Anthony Browne
Me and You

Farrar Straus Giroux

New York

For all the underdogs

Copyright © 2009 by Anthony Browne

All rights reserved

Originally published in France as *Une autre histoire* by Kaleidoscope, 2009

Published in Great Britain by Doubleday, an imprint of Random House Children's Books, 2010

Printed in January 2010 in Singapore by Tien Wah Press (Pte) Ltd.

First American edition, 2010

1 3 5 7 9 10 8 6 4 2

www.fsgkidsbooks.com

Library of Congress Cataloging-in-Publication Data

Browne, Anthony.

[Autre histoire. English]

Me and you / Anthony Browne.— 1st American ed.

p. cm.

Summary: An urban retelling of the classic Goldilocks and the Three Bears story, told from the baby bear's perspective.

ISBN: 978-0-374-34908-0 (alk. paper)

[1. Folklore.   2. Bears—Folklore.]   I. Title.

PZ8.1.B818Me 2010

398.2—dc22

[E]

2009032977

This is our house.

There's Daddy Bear, Mommy Bear, and me.

One morning Mommy made porridge for
breakfast, but it was too hot to eat.
"Let's all go out for a stroll in the park
while it cools down," said Daddy. So we did.

Daddy talked about *his* work and Mommy talked
about *her* work. I just messed around.

On the way back, Daddy talked about the car and
Mommy talked about the house. I just messed around.

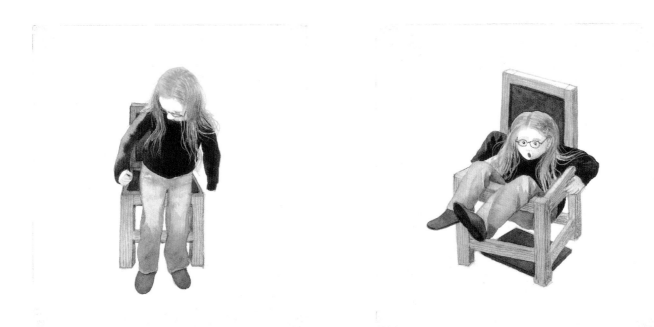

When we got home, the front door was open.
Daddy said that Mommy must have left it open,
and Mommy said it must have been Daddy.
I didn't say anything.

Daddy saw his spoon sticking out of his porridge.
"That's funny . . ." he said.
Mommy saw her spoon. "That's funny . . ." she said.
Then I saw that my bowl was empty. "That's not funny,"
I said. "Someone ate all my porridge."

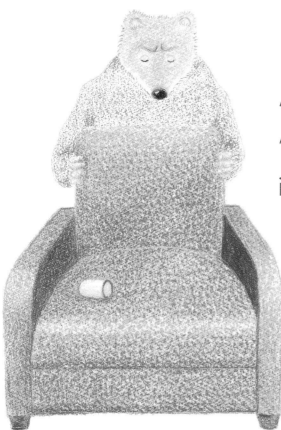

"Hang on a minute," said Daddy.
"Someone's been sitting
in my chair."

"Someone's been sitting
in MY chair!" said Mommy.

"Someone's been sitting in my chair
and they've BROKEN it!" I yelled.

"We'd better take a look upstairs,"
whispered Daddy. "After you, Mommy."

"Do be
careful,
dear,"
said
Daddy.

"Oh no," Daddy said. "SOMEONE'S been in my bed!"
"Oh!" shrieked Mommy. "Someone's been in MY bed!"
"Someone's been in my bed," I said, "and they're STILL THERE!"

The girl leaped out of bed and ran downstairs
and out the door.

I wonder what happened to her?